08-15

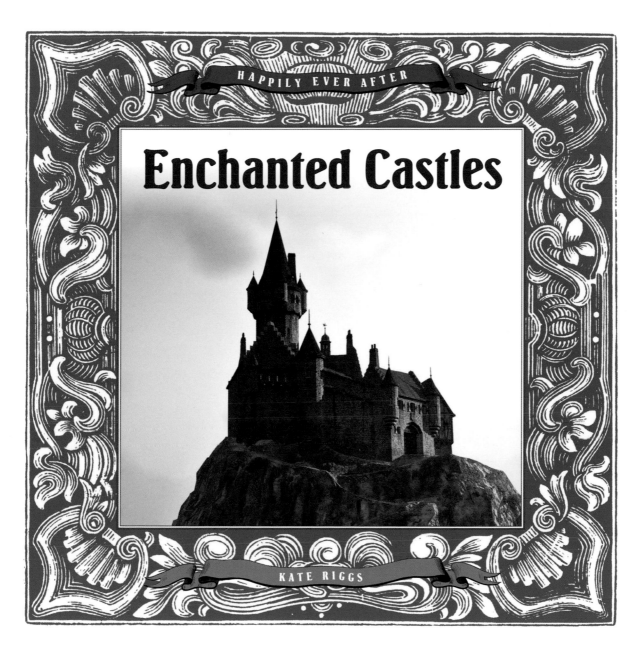

HAPPILY EVER AFTER

Enchanted Castles

KATE RIGGS

CREATIVE C EDUCATION

COPYRIGHT

Published by Creative Education
P.O. Box 227, Mankato, Minnesota 56002
Creative Education is an imprint of
The Creative Company
www.thecreativecompany.us

Design by Stephanie Blumenthal
Production by Christine Vanderbeek
Art direction by Rita Marshall
Printed in the United States of America

Photographs by by Alamy (AF archive, Mary Evans Picture Library, Pictorial Press Ltd), Dover Publications Inc. (120 Great Paintings from Medieval Illuminated Books; Castles; Historic Costume; Imps, Elves, Fairies & Goblins), Getty Images (Richard Eisermann), Graphic Frames (Agile Rabbit Editions), Shutterstock (Bob Orsillo, Unholy Vault Designs), SuperStock (James Steidl/SuperFusion), Wikipedia (John D. Batten, Viktor Vasnetsov)

Library of Congress Cataloging-in-Publication Data
Riggs, Kate.
Enchanted castles / by Kate Riggs.
p. cm. — (Happily ever after)
Summary: A primer of the familiar fairy-tale setting of enchanted castles, from what makes them spellbound to who inhabits them, plus famous stories and movies in which they have appeared.
Includes index.
ISBN 978-1-60818-240-4
1. Fairy tales. 2. Castles—Juvenile literature. I. Title.

GR550.R44 2013
398'.42—dc23   2011050867

First edition
9 8 7 6 5 4 3 2 1

TABLE OF CONTENTS

"*Once upon a time,
there was an* **enchanted** *castle.
It was in a dark forest.*"

Enchanted castles are places
you can find in fairy tales. A
fairy tale is a story about
magical people and places.

A castle is where a **royal** or rich family lives. Servants and other people live there, too. A castle becomes enchanted when someone puts a spell on it.

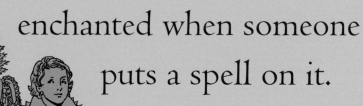

Enchanted castles can be hidden in magical forests. Some castles have magical gardens. Most enchanted castles have tall towers. They can be dark and scary places.

A wicked person puts a spell on a castle. That person might be an evil stepmother, a witch, or a bad fairy. Everyone who lives in the castle is also under the spell. Sometimes people are changed into animals.

❧ II ❧

There is only one person who can break the spell. That person is usually a prince or princess. It can take a long time for someone to break the spell.

A princess who is trapped in an enchanted castle needs a prince to save her. A prince under a spell needs a princess or other young lady to love him.

以下省略

Sleeping Beauty is a fairy tale about a beautiful princess who is put under a spell. She and everyone in her castle fall asleep for 100 years. A prince wakes her with a kiss.

The Disney movie *Beauty and the Beast* is about a girl named Belle. She stays in Beast's enchanted castle. Beast is scary and ugly. But Belle learns to love him. Belle's love turns Beast back into a handsome prince.

Everyone is made happy when an enchanted castle is freed from its spell.

"One day, a prince came to the enchanted castle. He fell in love with the princess. The spell was broken! And they all lived happily ever after."

Copy this short story onto a sheet of paper.
Then fill in the blanks with your own words!

Once upon a time, a princess named _____ lived in a castle called _____. The castle had _____ towers and _____ gardens. One day, a wicked witch named _____ cast a spell on Princess _____. The princess turned into a _____. Only a _____ could help her _____. The princess waited _____ years. Then a _____ came and _____ the spell! They lived happily ever after.

GLOSSARY

enchanted—put under a spell

royal—a king or queen or another member of their family

wicked—bad or evil

READ MORE

Casey, Jo, Beth Landis Hester, and Catherine Saunder. *The Princess Encyclopedia*. New York: DK Publishing, 2010.

Sims, Lesley. *The Enchanted Castle*. London: Usborne, 2007.

WEB SITES

Beauty and the Beast Coloring Pages
http://printables4kids.com/beauty-beast-printables/
Click on an activity or *Beauty and the Beast* coloring page to print it out.

Everything Sleeping Beauty
http://family.go.com/disney/pkg-disney-character-fun/pkg-everything-sleeping-beauty/
Have fun making crafts and treats that go along with the story of *Sleeping Beauty*.

INDEX